THE BIRTHDAY CAR

Margaret Hillert

Illustrated by Kelly Oechsli

MODERN CURRICULUM PRESS

Father said, "Come here.

Come here.

Run, run, run.

Come and find something."

7

Father said, "Look, look.

Here is something for you."

Oh, oh, oh.

A little red car.

I can go.

I can go away.

Away, away, away.

Oh, my.

Oh, my.

See me.

It is fun.

I can go up.

Up, up, up.

I can come down.

Down, down, down.

Here is a little blue car.

Come and play.

Here is a little yellow car.

Come and play.

Come and play.

One, two, three cars.

Three little cars.

Red, yellow, and blue.

Three little cars can go.

Away, away, away.

Away we go.

Oh, look.

Here is something.

Something big.

Come and play.

Look here, look here.

Here is something little.

It can go.

Come and play.

See something.

Come and play.

Here we go.

We can go up.

We can go down.

We can go to my house.

Father, Father.

Here we come.

Father said, "Come in.

Come in."

Oh, oh, oh.

A little red car is fun.

Margaret Hillert, author of several books in the MCP Beginning-To-Read Series, is a writer, poet, and teacher.

The Birthday Car
A beautifully illustrated, original story about a special birth-day present, told in just 39 preprimer words.

Word List

7 father	a	**12** up
said	little	**13** down
come	red	**14** blue
here	car	play
run	**10** I	**15** yellow
and	can	**16** one
find	go	two
something	away	three
8 look	**11** my	**17** we
is	see	**18** big
for	me	**24** to
you	it	house
9 oh	fun	**26** in